DeZert Isle

by Claude Ponti

translated by Mary Martin Holliday

David R. Godine · *Publisher* · *Boston*

For Adèle

First U.S. edition published in 2003 by
David R. Godine, Publisher
Post Office Box 450
Jaffrey, New Hampshire 03452
www.godine.com

Originally published in France
Copyright © 1999 by L'Ecole des loisirs
Translation copyright © 2003 by Mary Martin Holliday

LIBRARY OF CONGRESS
CATALOGING-IN-PUBLICATION DATA

Ponti, Claude
DeZert Isle / by Claude Ponti ;
translated by Mary Martin Holliday.—1st U.S. ed.
p.   cm.
Summary: A guided tour of sun-drenched
DeZert Isle, where Jules lives with the other
Zerts and his best friend, Ned the Nail.
ISBN 1-56792-237-6 (alk. paper)
[1. Islands—Fiction. 2. Friendship—Fiction.]
I. Holliday, Mary Martin. II. Title.
PZ7.P77258De2003
[E]—dc21   2002041664

FIRST U.S. EDITION
Printed in Spain

Jules is a Zert.

He lives on DeZert Isle. It's an island in the middle of the ocean, with water all around and sky up above.

Most of the time, the Zerts do what they always do. They run, climb, pile up on top of one another, fall down, jump up, and start all over again. The rest of the time, they do something else.

In the morning, Jules has breakfast with Ned the Nail.

Then he takes a shower up in the air.

Then, when he's quite clean…

… he goes and picks some flowers to offer to the Brick.

Jules is head-over-heels in love
with the Brick.

So, he needs lots and lots of flowers.

She is the only Brick on all of DeZert Isle. And she's the most beautiful brick of all. Jules is sure that she likes flowers, so he brings them for her every day.

And every day he tells her that his love is as big as a mountain on top of
a mountain and as deep as an ocean inside of an ocean.

One day Jules found a nail
along his path.

It was stuck in the grass
up to its nostrils.

It was Ned. He'd been stuck there for twenty-seven months and three days.
He had been attacked by SledgeHead.

Jules pulled with all his might...

... and yanked Ned out.

Ever since that day, Jules and Ned have been friends.
Sometimes they take a nap together. . .

. . . beside the sea. They make sand blankets, read a book or two,
and fall asleep while the breeze tickles their toes.

Jules hates SledgeHead. SledgeHead only has one thing on his mind: hammering nails. As soon as he sees one, he hammers it.

The worst is when he has one of his tantrums. Then he hammers everything that moves.

He doesn't stop until he's hammered everyone into the ground.

Jules also hates BigMouths. They spend their time swallowing everyone up.

If a Zert is walking in the forest thinking about something else...

. . . or looking at the leaves
on the trees. . .

. . . the BigMouth sneaks quietly
past him. . .

. . . and lies down in front of him, mouth wide open, well hidden in the green grass.

Then the Zert falls into his mouth. He has just enough time to say:
"Uh, oh! A BigMouth – I've got to jump over iiiiiiiiiiiiiiiiiiiiiiiiiiiiiiiiittt......"

He falls and falls...

... down onto a bunch of people.
And a bunch of people fall on him.

When the BigMouth gets too full, he explodes. It's the only way to get out. Then the BigMouth sticks himself back together all by himself and starts all over again.

But above all, Jules hates SmotherHen.

SmotherHen lies in wait,
high up in her nest.

As soon as she spies a Zert who's easy to catch, she dives.

She grabs him with her big feet and carries him away to try to hatch him.

She thinks that Zerts are her eggs.

When she's got one,
she sits on him forever.

ALL KINDS OF THINGS THAT JULES LOVES

Jules loves to tell the Brick
that he loves her.

Jules loves to pretend he's an ice cube
in a glass of fizzy water.

Jules loves to sleep beside a tortoise, and to drink hippopotamelon juice,

and to build walls, doors, and bridges with other Zerts.

He also loves to perform difficult balancing acts with Pyth and Goras.

And, most of all, he loves to offer bouquets of flowers to the Brick.

Sometimes he even likes to be scared a little bit.

Jules loves to peek into SmotherHen's nest, just in case
she's trying to hatch some poor Zert.

At night, he loves to watch the stars
race across the sky.

And, even more than that, he loves to offer
a hippopotamelon to the Brick.

Jules loves to be very brave and play tricks on SledgeHead.

He lets SledgeHead chase him up to a Zert wall...

... and watches SledgeHead crash into it. If the "Splattt!!!" is big enough, Jules is the winner, and then it's another Zert's turn to be brave.

Jules loves to feed the Flying Carpettes
from a branch of the blue palm.

And, even more, he loves
to offer sausages to the Brick.

One day when SledgeHead missed Ned,
Jules got hammered on the head instead.

Jules was all wibbly-wobbly.   Completely wibbly-wobbly.

So very wibbly-wobbly...   ...that he fell right over.

When he woke up, he saw the Brick.
He thought she was so beautiful,

so straight, so square, that right away
he fell head-over-heels in love with her.

He talked about her for hours. Everyone listened to him with delight.
Everyone, that is, except a little Zert named Romeotte.

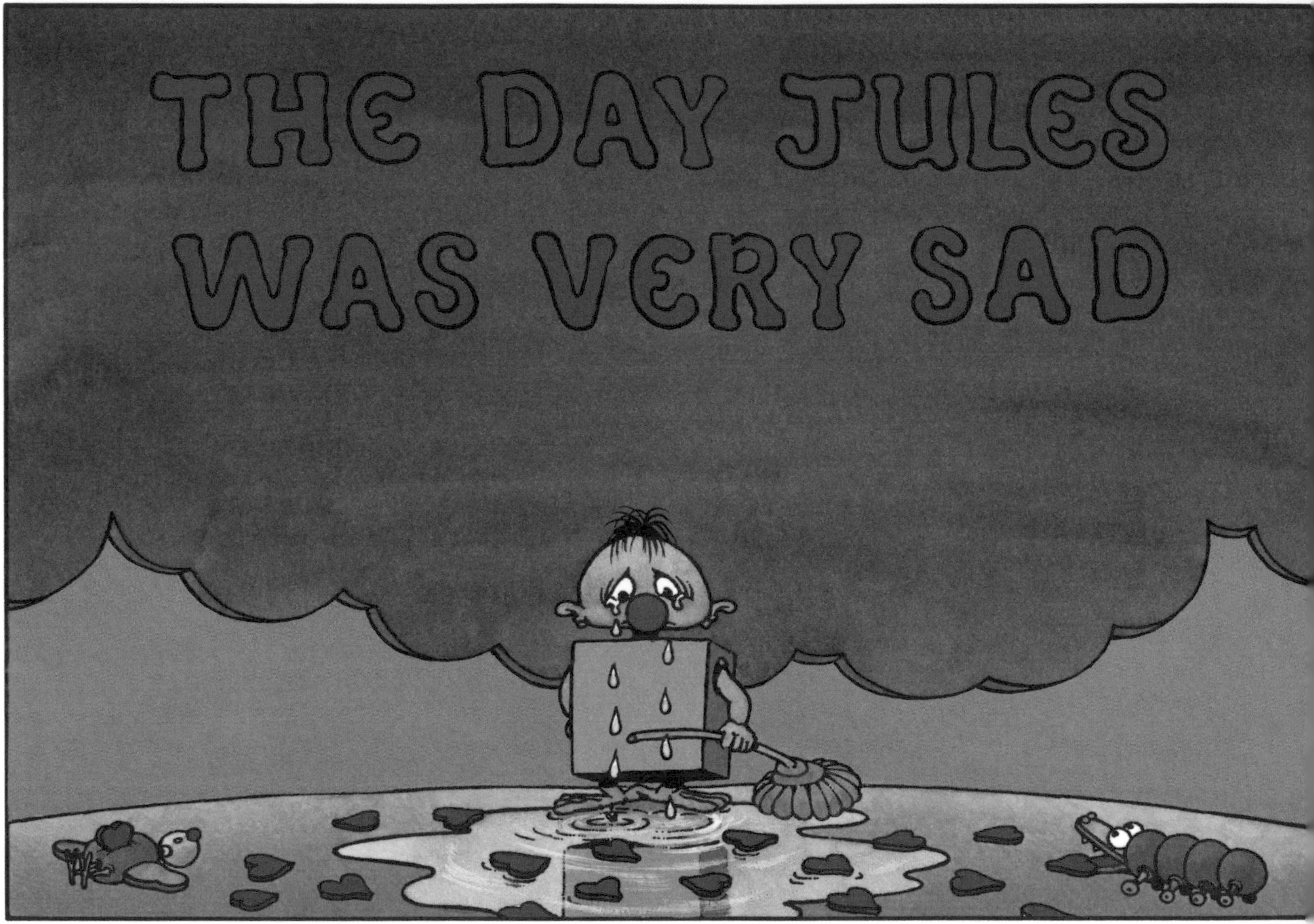
THE DAY JULES
WAS VERY SAD

The day Jules was very sad was
the day when he asked . . .

. . . the Brick if she would like
to marry him.

A Gardener said to him: "She won't answer you. Don't you see that she never answers you? She doesn't love you! Besides, she has no heart, and I should know, because I'm the one who planted her here."

Jules went away. All around him was
the deZert.

He sat down, and cried
until he had no tears left.

Much later, SledgeHead was trying to hammer Ned
for the one hundred and twenty-fifth time...

. . . and for the one hundred and twenty-fifth time, Jules and Ned were running away, while . .

. . . not far away, a BigMouth was sneaking quietly past Romeotte to swallow her.

Jules and Ned jumped oooooOOOOOOover the BigMouth. SledgeHead. . .

. . . fell down inside. And Jules ran into Romeotte.

They were a little wibbly-wobbly,
and they knew they were really in love.

Ned ran into Oum-Djazoume,
and the sun ran into the moon.

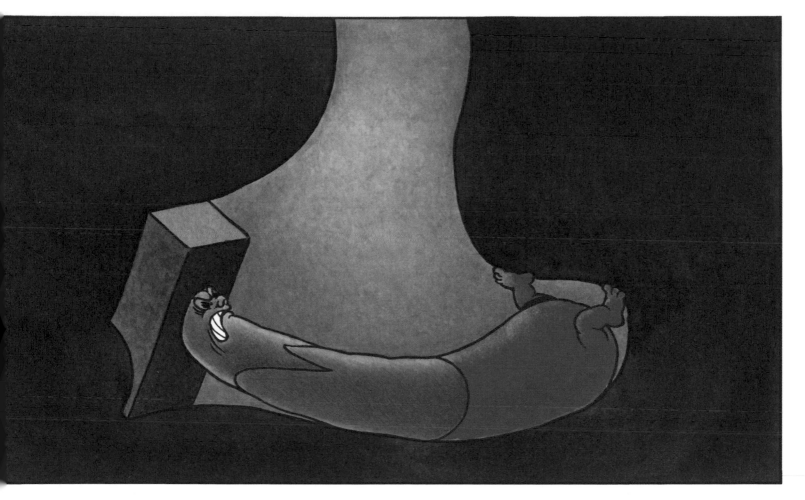

At the bottom of the BigMouth, SledgeHead didn't run into anyone.

Jules and Romeotte closed off the BigMouth. And they gave each other kisses.

After two million kisses, they left, and everywhere they went, everyone was happy, and the really grumpy people went away to be completely forgotten on another island.

This is how Jules and Romeotte met. And every night since then, they watch the stars race across the sky together.